DATE DUE		6/15
1/5/19			

Facing a Frenemy

by: Jan Fields
Illustrated by: Tracy Bishop

visit us at www.abdopublishing.com

Published by Magic Wagon, a division of the ABDO Group,
PO Box 398166, Minneapolis, MN 55439. Copyright © 2014 by
Abdo Consulting Group, Inc. International copyrights reserved
in all countries. All rights reserved. No part of this book may
be reproduced in any form without written permission from the
publisher.

Calico Chapter Books™ is a trademark and logo of Magic Wagon.

Printed in the United States of America, North Mankato, Minnesota.
102013
012014

Written by Jan Fields
Illustrated by Tracy Bishop
Edited by Stephanie Hedlund and Rochelle Baltzer
Cover and interior design by Renée LaViolette

Library of Congress Cataloging-in-Publication Data

Fields, Jan, author.
  Facing a frenemy / by Jan Fields ; illustrated by Tracy Bishop.
     pages cm. -- (Meri's mirror)
  Summary: Meri is puzzled and hurt because her former best friend
has turned on her--but when she is given a magic mirror by her aunt
she gets some help in sorting out the problem from Anne of Green
Gables.
  ISBN 978-1-62402-008-7
1. Shirley, Anne (Fictitious character)--Juvenile fiction. 2. Best
friends--Juvenile fiction. 3. Friendship--Juvenile fiction. 4. Magic
mirrors--Juvenile fiction. 5. Elementary schools--Juvenile fiction.
[1. Best friends--Fiction. 2. Friendship--Fiction. 3. Magic--Fiction.
4. Mirrors--Fiction. 5. Shirley, Anne (Fictitious character)--Fiction.
6. Characters in literature--Fiction. 7. Schools--Fiction.] I. Bishop,
Tracy, illustrator. II. Title.
  PZ7.F479177Fac 2014
  813.6--dc23
                                              2013025336

Table of Contents

A Package

Meredith Mercer tromped down the stairs. At the bottom, she turned right. She stepped over the backpacks and sweaters piled on the floor. When she reached the worn couch, she sat between stacks of clean clothes that were ready to be put away. Her eyes stayed on the pages of her book the whole time.

"Meri, you should watch when you walk," her mother said as she passed through the room on the way to her office. "You could fall."

"Yes, Mom," Meri said without looking up. She was at the best part of her favorite book, *Anne of Green Gables.* "I could never express all my sorrow," Meri read in a whisper. "No, not if I used up the whole dictionary. You must just imagine it."

"Are you reading that old book again?" Meri's sister Judith groaned. She picked up a pile of clean clothes and balanced it on another pile so she could sit on the couch. "I'll go to the library with you if you need a new book."

Meri shook her head. "I like rereading books."

Judith snorted. "I never reread. The library is full of new books. I could never read them all. If I reread a book, I might miss a really good new one."

Meri knew this was true. And she did worry about that sometimes. But she couldn't give up her old books. She loved them. They were like visiting friends.

Judith stretched her long legs out in front of the couch. "So, is Kaylin still being awful at school?"

Meri sighed and closed her book. "She said my hair looks like a nest. She stuck a plastic egg in it. It fell out and rolled across my worktable. Everyone laughed."

Judith nodded. "I heard all about my egghead sister. I figured Kaylin was behind that."

Meri moaned. If sixth graders were talking about it, then everyone in the whole world knew.

"What happened with you and Kaylin?" Judith asked. "You two used to do everything together."

"I don't know," Meri said. "She doesn't talk to me anymore, except to say mean things."

"Do you want me to talk to her?" Judith asked, a frown squinting her eyes.

Part of Meri wanted to say yes. Judith could be scary. And Meri really wanted Kaylin to stop being so mean. But Meri remembered when Kaylin was her friend. They read the same books. They hated the same icky food. And Kaylin always made Meri laugh. Why couldn't she have that back?

Loud bangs and clumps came from the stairs. Judith and Meri turned. The twins almost tumbled into the room.

"Someone's coming!" Kat shouted.

"With a package!" Thomas shouted even louder.

Judith unfolded from the couch like a lamb standing on long, wobbly legs. She headed toward the door and Meri followed her.

The pounding on the front door made it rattle. Things rattled at Meri's house a lot. The house was really big and really old. Sometimes Meri's mom carried a toolbox into one of the shakier rooms and pounded for a while. Sometimes that made things better. Sometimes not.

Judith hauled open the door. A man in a brown uniform pushed a big box into her arms. Judith took the package with an *oomph*. The man waved his clipboard.

"Sign here," he said.

"With what?" Judith asked as she tried to shift her grip on the box.

"I'll sign it," Meri offered.

The man looked over Meredith's head, clearly hoping a grown-up would appear. Finally, he sighed and shoved the clipboard into her hands. "Sign here," he said.

Meri signed on the line. She was very proud of her handwriting. She liked the loops and humps and swooping tails in her name. The man didn't even look at her signature. He just grabbed the clipboard and ordered her to have a nice day. Then he turned and ran down the front steps.

Judith heaved the box to the floor beside the piano. She peered at the address label. "It's for you, Meri," she said. "It's from Aunt Prudence."

"It's a birthday present," Kat said. "A big one."

Meri looked at the box. It might be a birthday present. Her birthday was over a month ago, but Aunt P never got things quite right.

"Mom! Meri got a present!" Thomas yelled, racing from the room. Kat ran behind him.

"So, are you going to open it?" Judith asked, nudging the box with her knee. "I would have had this thing open so fast."

Meri knelt and began carefully peeling the tape from the box. She heard Judith making irritated huffy noises over her head. Finally,

Meri pulled off the last piece of tape and opened the flaps of the box. Yards of Bubble Wrap covered a shadowy object inside.

"Bubble Wrap!" The twins were back in the room, shrieking.

Meri pulled the thickly wrapped object from the box. It was heavy. She thought it must be some kind of picture from the shape. As she pulled off each sheet of Bubble Wrap, one of the twins would grab it and leap on it.

Soon the room rang with the sound of tiny bubble explosions. Meri looked down at her gift. It was a mirror. Why would Aunt P send her a mirror? Maybe she confused Meri with Kat. Her little sister loved looking at herself in the mirror. Didn't Aunt P remember that Meri was more into books than looks?

Movie Night

"Oh Meredith, it's beautiful," Mom said. She stepped around the twins. They had begun laying the Bubble Wrap sheets on the floor so they could jump on them. The noise was almost painful.

Mom picked up the mirror and held it at arm's length. "We can hang it over your desk," she said. "It will be like having a vanity."

Kat stopped jumping. "A what?"

"A vanity is where you sit and stare at yourself," Judith said.

"I want a vanity," Kat wailed.

Mom patted her youngest daughter on the head. "When you're older. And you do not simply sit and stare at yourself. It's where you prepare to look your best each day."

"You could put it in Kat's room," Meri said. "I wouldn't mind."

Mom beamed at Meri. "That's very generous. But this is yours. Besides, you're at the perfect age to start spending more time on your appearance."

Judith snickered. Mom only gave her the look and headed upstairs, still holding the mirror out like a shield.

Meri sighed. Goodie. She would love having something hanging on her wall to remind her that she had crazy hair puffed around her boring, round face.

Mom quickly hung the mirror. Then she began picking up the books scattered over the desk.

"You should keep these in your bookcase," Mom said. "Then you'll have room for some hair things."

"I have all the hair things I need," Meri said.

"I could get you some fingernail polish," Mom said. "And some new headbands."

Meri moaned.

Mom snapped her fingers. "Lip gloss. I'm sure Judith was wearing lip gloss at your age."

"I have a lip balm," Meri said. "That's plenty."

"I should make a list and go to the store," Mom said. She was still naming things off as she left the room.

Meri sagged in her desk chair. She laid *Anne of Green Gables* in the middle of the empty desktop. It looked lonely without all of Meri's other favorites.

She made faces at herself in her new mirror. "Anne wouldn't like looking at herself all the time," Meri said. "And neither do I!"

Meri's reflection had no advice for her. Instead, she pulled her book toward her and went back to reading about Anne's dramatic apology scene. Meri loved imagining herself doing over-the-top things like Anne Shirley.

She didn't look up again until Thomas yelled up the stairs that it was supper time.

After supper, she listened to Thomas and Kat read for their reading logs. Judith said she was walking to the library to check out a movie.

"No dressed-up lady movies!" Thomas yelled.

"No sup titles!" Kat yelled.

"Subtitles," Meri corrected. Then she tapped the page in Kat's book.

Kat rolled her eyes at Meri, but she started reading again.

When Judith came back with the movie, their sister Hannah followed her in.

"Ah," Dad said. "All the Mercers have come home to roost."

He said the same thing every night when Hannah got home. Hannah played almost every sport the high school had. That meant she was always home last. Hannah squeezed onto the couch beside Dad. The twins scrambled over to climb on them both.

Meri headed into the kitchen, where Mom was sipping a cup of tea.

"Hannah's home," Meri said. "And Judith is back with the movie."

Mom smiled. "Great. Can you get the popcorn?"

Tuesday night was always movie night at their house. Mom said it was because too many families only do fun stuff on the weekends. "Homework is important," she said. "But so is fun."

Meri dragged the kitchen step stool from the narrow space between the counter and the fridge. She used it to reach the microwave popcorn in the upper cabinet. She tore the plastic wrapper off the popcorn and read the directions. The directions were always the same, but Meri believed in being careful.

Soon wild popping started in the microwave and the smell of hot popcorn filled the kitchen. Judith came in to pour drinks.

"What movie did you get?" Mom asked.

Judith hauled the gallon jug of apple juice from the fridge. She lowered it to the counter with a thud. "*Pride and Prejudice.*"

Meri laughed. "Thomas will be thrilled."

Judith shrugged. "We watched *Sherlock Holmes* last week. That was a guy movie."

"It was the old BBC version," Meri said. "You know how Thomas feels about costumes."

Another shrug. "They weren't lady costumes."

"Thomas still complained."

Judith waved her hand as if shooing the complaints away. "Thomas complains a lot."

"If you were the only boy with four sisters," Mom said, "you'd complain too."

The movie turned out to be good. Meri thought Mr. Darcy was awfully mean at first. She wasn't sure she would forgive him like Elizabeth Bennet did.

"That's because you're too young to understand," Judith said. Her voice was all prissy and grown up. Meri hated when she did that voice.

"I'm older than you, Judith," Hannah said. "And I wouldn't have let him off the hook so easy either."

Thomas had fallen asleep, leaning against the tower of laundry. Dad scooped him up and carried him to bed. Kat collapsed on the floor and pretended she was asleep, too. When Dad came back down, he tickled her until she giggled. Then he sent everyone up to bed.

"Grab your laundry on the way," Mom said. "You guys have spent enough time ignoring it."

When Meri turned off her light for bed, she glanced toward the mirror. In the dim light, her image looked like a ghost in a long, pale gown.

"I look even scarier in the dark," she muttered, then climbed into bed.

She overslept a little in the morning and had to hurry to get ready. She never even glanced at her new mirror as she rushed. Finally, she grabbed her book from the desk. She looked toward the mirror and froze.

A girl looked back at her, clutching her own copy of *Anne of Green Gables*. But she wasn't Meredith Mercer. She wasn't Meri at all!

Anne Shirley

Meri stared at the girl in the mirror. The girl stared back. The girl in the mirror had long, red hair in thick braids. Her dress was a strange yellowish-grey color. Her face was small, like Meri's, but thin and covered with freckles. Her eyes were huge.

"Who are you?" Meri whispered.

The girl leaned forward and peered at Meri.

"Who are you?" Meri repeated.

The girl watched Meri intently as she spoke. Then she smiled, pointed at herself, and answered. Only Meri didn't hear a thing.

"What?" Meri asked, speaking a bit louder now.

The girl opened her mouth wide and spoke again, clearly shouting this time. Meri didn't hear anything. Finally, they simply stared at each other. Then the girl's face lit up. She held up the book that looked exactly like Meri's own book. The girl pointed at the title and then at herself.

Meri opened her eyes wide in surprise. She pulled a sheet of paper out of her desk drawer and wrote on it quickly with a marker. She held it up. *You're Anne Shirley?*

The girl in the mirror smiled widely. She nodded.

Meri wrote her own name on the paper and held it up. She pointed at herself.

Anne nodded back and mouthed the name.

By now, Meri realized Aunt Prudence had sent her a magic mirror. It must be showing her Anne Shirley because the book sat alone under the mirror all night. It was just the kind of exciting thing Meri always dreamed would happen.

Except in Meri's dreams, they would be able to hear each other.

Meri bent over her desk and wrote some more. She held up the new note. *Are you at Green Gables?*

Anne read the question, then looked around her in surprise. From what Meri could see, Anne was in a room exactly like Meri's. Anne looked back at her and shook her head. She mouthed something else, but Meri couldn't quite tell what it was. From the look on Anne's face, Meri guessed she didn't know where she was.

Meri bent to scribble another question. "Can you move around or are you stuck in the mirror?"

Anne read the question. Then she stepped back from the mirror and began to march around the room. Meri blinked. As strange as it was to find Anne in the mirror, it was stranger still to see her march around the room.

Finally, Anne marched back up to the mirror and mouthed, "Nice room."

"Thanks," Meri said.

They smiled at each other for a minute. Meri wished there was some way she could hear Anne. What good was a magic mirror if you couldn't hear the other person?

Suddenly Anne leaned over. Meri could see the straight part at the top of her head. Finally, Anne popped back up and held up a paper of her own. It was covered in words.

What wonderful writing paper. It's so smooth, like glass. And the drawer has these lovely pens in every color. You don't even have to dip them in an ink bottle. I love them. I could draw pictures all day long. It's a wonder you get anything else done at all. Do tell me if I should call you Meredith or Mary or Dithy. Oh, how silly that sounds. I know you're not a Dithy. I am absolutely sure we can be bosom friends. Even if you are imaginary. I've had imaginary friends before. But none I could see so clearly. I do have one bosom friend, Diana, but she doesn't live inside a mirror. Do you think you can like me a little—enough to be my bosom friend?

Meredith blinked at the long note. She had nearly forgotten just how much Anne loved words. Plus, she was nearly certain the last line was exactly what Anne had said in the book when she met Diana.

Meri bent over to write a reply. She held up her note. *I'd like to be friends. I'm not imaginary. You can call me Meredith or Meri.*

Anne's face lit up. She bent over again for another long moment. Meri smiled. She imagined how full this second note would be.

Anne straightened up. This time she had written each sentence in her note with a different color.

I'm so glad you aren't imaginary. Are you magic? I love magic. I can't do any, of course, but I love thinking about it. Do you like imagining? It makes everything so much better. When all the very worst things happen, you can simply imagine yourself into something totally different.

"Meredith Mercer!" Mom's voice boomed up the stairs. "Come down here and eat your breakfast."

Meri looked over at the clock. Oh no. She was going to be so late. She scribbled a quick note and held it up. *I'll see you after school. I have to go. I think it's the mirror that's magic —I'm just ordinary. I'll come straight back after school.*

Anne nodded at her. Meri put her book carefully back on the desk in case Anne needed it to stay in the mirror. Then she grabbed her backpack and rushed downstairs.

"You're going to have to eat fast," Judith said when Meri slipped into a chair and grabbed a box of cereal.

Meri nodded. She poured cereal and milk. As she shoveled the cereal into her mouth, she thought about her magic mirror. She hoped Anne would still be there when she got home.

"Listen," Judith whispered. "Don't let Kaylin make you scared of going to school."

Meri looked at her sister in surprise. "I'm not," she mumbled around the cereal in her mouth. Kaylin made her feel sad and upset. She hated the mean things Kaylin said. But she wasn't really afraid.

Judith looked doubtful. "If you want me to talk to her, just say so."

Meri shook her head hard. Then Mom called for everyone to get in the van. Meri shoved one more spoonful of cereal into her mouth. Then she grabbed a piece of cold toast to eat in the van.

Meri wished Judith hadn't reminded her about Kaylin. She shifted her backpack onto her shoulder and headed for the door. As she walked, she wondered, *What would Anne Shirley do about a bully like Kaylin?*

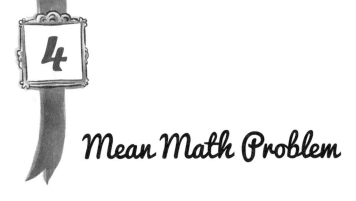

Mean Math Problem

Meredith unzipped her backpack and pulled out her lunch. She shoved it into the small cubby over her peg in the coat closet. Then she rooted in her backpack for her book before remembering that she left it under the mirror, under Anne.

The classroom library covered the bottom half of one whole wall. Most of the books were a little shabby, but Meri didn't mind that. It helped her pick. The best books always had missing corners on the covers and rumpled pages.

She spotted one book with a spine partly peeled away and grabbed it. It was *A Wrinkle in Time*. Meri had never read it, but she liked the title. She wondered if her magic mirror did something like that. Did it create a wrinkle in time that let her talk to Anne? Meri shook her head. The mirror had to do more than wrinkle time. Anne wasn't even a real person!

"I can't believe you need another book." The mocking voice pulled Meri's attention back to the classroom. She turned to look at Kaylin. Her ex-best friend stood with her hands on her hips. Beside her stood Kaylin's two new best friends in meanness, Gina and Megan.

"Oh look," Kaylin's friend Megan said. "I see a smear on your nose, Meri-dip. It must be ink from rubbing it on the book pages."

"I don't have ink on my nose," Meri said, rubbing at the end of her nose anyway.

"Her skin is just naturally pale," Gina said. "From reading books in her cave."

"I don't live in a cave," Meri said.

"No, she lives in a rickety old house," Kaylin said with a laugh. "It looks like something from a horror movie!"

Meri's house was old, but her dad kept the lawn mowed and her mom planted flowers in boxes all over. It didn't look anything like a haunted house. "You know that's not true!"

Kaylin opened her eyes wide. "Are you calling me a liar?"

"Ooooohhhhh!" her mean friends said together.

Meri crossed her arms and glared at Kaylin. "My house doesn't look bad and you know it."

"I know I wouldn't go in it again," Kaylin said. "It might fall down with me inside."

"You aren't invited in anyway," Meri said. Then she turned with her book clutched to her chest and stormed over to her seat. Kaylin and her friends started after her, but Mrs. Miller told them to find their own seats.

Meredith flipped through the pages in the book, but inside she was full of storms. She wanted to stand up and yell at Kaylin for being so mean. She didn't though. Meri didn't really like fighting. It felt good when she was yelling, but when she thought about it later, she always felt awful.

She blinked back tears. Why couldn't things go back to the way they were when Kaylin was her friend? Sure, Gina and Megan were mean even then, but it didn't feel so bad when she wasn't alone. Today, she had the best secret in the whole world and no best friend to tell it to.

Mrs. Miller was one of Meredith's favorite people in the world. She was full of interesting stories and new things to try. One of their morning warm-ups every day was writing story problems for Mrs. Miller to solve. She called it her homework. The only rule was that you had to know the answer for the problem you wrote. You wrote your answer at the bottom and covered it with a sticker.

Sometimes Meri's answer didn't match Mrs. Miller's answer. Her teacher always "showed her work" so Meri could tell where she made

her mistake. Even when Meri's answer was wrong, she always got the "good story" sticker.

Meredith sighed as she looked down at her story problem sheet for the day. Her heart was so sad, she had trouble thinking of an interesting math problem. Finally, she decided to just do the one that bothered her most. She picked up her pencil and tilted her paper so her left hand wouldn't get smudged as she wrote.

"Rachel's class had two mean girls and one nice girl. The nice girl was Rachel's best friend. When the nice girl turned mean, the class had three mean girls. Why does two plus one feel like such a big number?"

Meri sighed. She knew it didn't sound like a real math problem, but it was the only one she could think of. Still, she needed a real math problem. She turned her pencil around to erase what she'd written.

"Please, pass your morning work to the front," Mrs. Miller said.

With no time to change her problem, Meri wrote, "I don't know" in the answer space and covered it with the sticker. Then she passed her sheet to the front and slumped in her seat. Now, Mrs. Miller was probably going to be mad at her, too.

Because Maxwell Meyer Elementary School didn't have a cafeteria, all the students ate at their desks. When they were done, they could go outside and play until lunchtime was over. Most kids ate really fast.

Ever since Kaylin turned mean, Meri had eaten lunch really slow. It was lonely being outside with no friend. After she was finished, she gathered her trash and threw it away. Then she settled back into her seat and opened up *A Wrinkle in Time.*

"Don't you want to go outside and play?" Mrs. Miller asked.

Meri shook her head. "I'm at a really exciting part of this book."

Mrs. Miller got up from her desk and walked over to sit in one of the chairs at Meri's worktable. She held Meri's morning work in her hand.

"I'm sorry about the math problem," Meri said. "I know it was stupid."

"There's nothing about you or your work that's stupid," Mrs. Miller said. "And you know I'm not fond of that word."

"Sorry," Meri said.

"If these girls are being mean to you, I can talk to them," Mrs. Miller said. "I don't want you to feel afraid to go out for recess."

"I'm not afraid," Meri said. "Really. They say mean things but it's not that big of a deal. Gina and Megan have always been like that."

"Well, probably not always," Mrs. Miller said. "But it's my job to make sure no one is being bullied."

"It's okay," Meri said with a sigh. "I just don't understand why Kaylin wants to hang out with them and act like them."

"Sometimes friends grow apart," Mrs. Miller said.

Meri almost rolled her eyes like Judith, but she knew Mrs. Miller was trying to help. Still, that was such a grown-up thing to say. Meri looked down at her book.

"You know, I'm glad you're such a good reader. I loved books when I was your age, too," Mrs. Miller said. "But sometimes you have to look around to see good things that are there."

That didn't make all that much sense either, but because she liked Mrs. Miller, Meri looked up and smiled. "I'll try that."

Mrs. Miller patted her arm and stood up. "Then I think you'll be just fine. But if things don't get better, you need to tell me. You need to let me help."

Meri nodded.

Mall Madness

Meredith didn't just think about the mean girls at school. She also thought about the problem with Anne. How could she make a mirror talk? If it was like yelling to someone through a wall, she should have been able to hear something. She sometimes yelled to Judith through the walls, and her sister always heard her. Plus, a mirror was a lot thinner than a wall.

When the class was divided into their reading groups, Meri looked at the other kids in her group. She didn't really know them that well. She just knew they could all read hard books like her. Right now they were reading a Time Warp Trio book because it was David's turn to pick.

"My favorite part of the book so far is the magic book that takes them places," Jasmine said shyly. Then she dropped her eyes and almost put one of her braids in her mouth. Meri remembered that Jasmine chewed on her hair sometimes. Maybe she was trying to quit.

"Magic books are okay," David said. "But I like it because it's funny."

"Don't you like magic stuff?" Meri asked.

David shrugged. "I like real stuff better. You know, computers, smart phones, MP3 players. I saw this cool thing at the mall last night. You put it on anything and it turns the thing into a speaker. The guy did it with a pizza box. It was amazing."

Jasmine giggled quietly. "A singing pizza box."

David grinned. "Right, isn't that better than magic?"

"Do you think that would work with a mirror?" Meri asked.

"I guess." David shrugged.

"How much did it cost?"

"Twenty dollars."

Meri had twenty dollars. She liked to save her Christmas and birthday money until she saw something really special. This speaker sounded like it might be just what she needed to talk to Anne.

After school, Meri ran right home and up to her room. She was suddenly afraid that

she'd find an ordinary mirror hanging on her wall. When she rushed through the door and looked into the smiling face of Anne Shirley, she laughed in relief.

She pulled a sheet of paper out of her drawer and wrote quickly. *I may have found a way to help us talk.*

Anne's face lit up even brighter as she read the note. It took a bit longer to write her reply. *That is the most glorious news I've ever heard. I've been trying to come up with a plan all day. I thought about some kind of tapping code, but I do not know if that would truly be better than writing notes. It would be mysterious and secret though, don't you think?*

I'm not sure. Meri wrote. *But I do think I might have the way. I have to go to the mall, but I'll be back soon.*

What's a mall? Anne wrote.

Meri thought about that for a moment. How do you explain a mall to someone who has never seen one? *It's a really big store full of little stores inside.*

Is it far away? Anne wrote.

Too far to walk. I'm going to get my mom to drive me.

Anne nodded. *How grand that your mother drives your buggy. Matthew always drives ours, but I don't think he really likes going anywhere.*

Meri nodded. She always felt she understood Matthew and his desire to stay away from the attention of others. She'd rather be home too. She thought about telling Anne that, but decided to wait until they could talk for real.

She wrote, *Be back soon.* Then she waved while Anne waved back wildly.

Meri dashed down the stairs and nearly plowed into her mother, who stood at the bottom with a clothes basket in her arms. "Don't run on the stairs," her mom scolded. "What's your rush?"

"I need to go to the mall, right away."

Mom smiled. "A mall emergency? I thought you'd be a bit older before you had one of those. Meeting friends?"

Meri wrinkled her nose at the silly idea. "No, I need to buy something."

"For a school assignment?"

"No," Meri admitted. "But I'll be spending my own money. It's something I need."

"Clothes?" Mom said hopefully.

"Speakers."

Her mom looked at her in confusion. "But you don't listen to music."

Meri ran through possible answers. She had an MP3 player but she never played music. She played talking books that she downloaded from the library. And she listened to them with her earbuds.

"Sometimes my earbuds hurt my ears," she said honestly. "And if I had speakers, I could play my MP3 player in my room without the earbuds."

Her mom nodded. "Okay, let me grab these dirty towels for your dad." Meri's dad liked loading the big washer and dryer. He liked the precision of folding clothes. But he hated gathering them up, especially since the twins tended to leave stray towels under their beds. So her mom and dad split the laundry chores.

Meri followed along behind her, almost dancing with impatience. Finally, Mom gathered her keys and they headed to the mall. At the mall, she practically dragged her pokey mom down the center where the kiosks lined up. When she reached the speaker kiosk, the man was showing a few passing people how a small circle with a cord could turn his kiosk into a speaker.

"Would that work with a mirror?" she asked.

"Yes, it would," he said.

"Then I'll take one."

6

A New Bosom Friend

Meri carefully counted out her money while her mom frowned slightly.

Her mother leaned forward and whispered to Meri, "There are much cheaper speakers you can get for your MP3."

"I know," Meri said. "But my new mirror will make a great speaker."

Meri's mom sighed. She always let them make their own decisions about their money, and she was usually happy with Meri's careful decisions. Meri was sorry to make her mom sigh, but she just had to talk to Anne.

She tightly clutched the plastic bag with the speaker package all the way home. Meri burst out of the car before her mom even turned off the engine. She ran for the house.

Once she got to her room, she pulled the pieces of the speaker out of the box. She had a cord that plugged into a cylinder that she attached to the mirror. The other end of the cord had a plug.

"I hope this works," Meri said. She caught Anne's questioning expression and offered

her a smile. Then she pushed the plug into the wall.

"Can you hear me?" she asked.

Anne's eyes opened wide. "I can," she said. Meri heard her response clearly. Her voice sounded exactly the way Meri imagined, full of life and excitement.

"It worked," Meri said.

"You are brilliant," Anne said, her hands clasped. "I am simply the luckiest orphan in the world to have such a brilliant new friend."

Meri laughed as she remembered Mrs. Miller telling her to look up to see good things. She was looking up at her new best friend, who definitely was not saying mean things.

"Thank you," she said. "I'm glad to get to talk to you. This has been a day of big ups and big downs."

"I do hope I was one of the ups," Anne said.

"The up-est."

Anne laughed. "I don't believe I know that word. I love new words and today I have two:

mall and *up-est.*"

"Well, malls are real. But I made up the other word."

"Oh, I love to make up words," Anne said. "I especially love naming things and places. When I first met Matthew, we were walking on the Avenue. It was beautiful. I needed a beautiful name. So I called it 'White Way of Delight.' Isn't that a nice, imaginative name?"

"I like it," Meri said with a laugh.

"Please, my dear friend, tell me all about your day."

Meri sat down in her chair and told Anne everything. Sometimes Anne gasped and opened her eyes so wide that Meredith had an alarming worry about them falling right out of her small face. Once, Anne even reached out as if to grab Meri's hand, but her fingers just crashed against the glass.

"Oh, that was quite painful," Anne said, hugging her fingers to her chest.

"I'm so sorry," Meri said sympathetically. "I wish you were here with me. I'd get you some ice for it."

"Oh?" Anne's eyes widened in excitement again. "Is it winter there?"

"No, I would just get it from the freezer."

"Freezer," Anne repeated carefully. "You have some tool that freezes things. How very useful."

Meri had to agree. She couldn't imagine trying to live without a freezer, but she guessed Anne would know all about that. She lived without television or computers or MP3 players, too.

"What did you do all day?" Meri asked.

"I read some of your wonderful books," Anne said. She turned in her seat to point behind her where Meredith's bookcase stood against the wall in the mirror room. The mirror bookcase was just as cram-packed with books as the real bookcase. "And I drew pictures with the beautiful pens."

"Did you get bored?"

"Oh, no, it was lovely," Anne said. "Only I can't actually leave this room. I missed going outside. I do love to be outside where I can see flowers and hear birds sing."

"I wonder if you would be able to go back outside if I took away the book from the desk," Meri said. "You could go back to your beloved Green Gables."

"I would like to go back," Anne admitted. "But not right now. We've barely met each other, and I've been wanting a bosom friend for ever so long. And your room has shown me that we are going to be the best of friends. Only a person of great imagination would have so many books of amazing stories. Have you read all the books?"

"In the bookcase? Yes, sometimes more than once."

"Oh good. I have so many questions about them. But first, I do think we need to talk more about the situation with this Kaylin person. I do like her name. It's mysterious and exotic, though not nearly as elegant as Cordelia. That's my favorite name. Don't you think that's much nicer than Anne? But oh, we were talking about Kaylin. Is she your nemesis?"

"Nemesis?" Meri echoed.

"Your evil match," Anne said. "The enemy you battle bravely."

"Not exactly," Meri said. "She used to be my best friend, but now she's mean to me all the time."

"Why did she change?" Anne asked.

Meri shook her head. "I don't know."

"Why don't you ask her? Then you can know. You might have done something to offend her without knowing it. All you will need to do is apologize once you know." Anne's eyes grew big and round. "I can help you with that. I love planning apologies. I didn't think

I would until I tried, but they're one of the most wonderful things."

Again Meri laughed, remembering Anne's passionate apology in the book. "But you didn't even mean that apology to Mrs. Rachel Lynde."

"Oh, you're wrong. I did. I meant it with all my heart. I was in agony from what I had done." Anne's voice rose to its theatrical best.

"I can probably handle the apology if I did anything wrong," Meri said. "But she's the one who's been mean."

"It was the same way with Mrs. Rachel Lynde. She said horrible things about me, as you might remember. And what I said to her was totally true. Like you, I felt that I could not be sorry, but when I thought about it, I was. I thought about what a terrible, wicked girl I had been. I thought of how I had hurt Marilla. And I thought of how I didn't deserve all the lovely things at Green Gables. I just thought and thought until I felt the sorrow in my toes.

Everything was better when I apologized. Though, of course, you should find out what you did wrong. It makes the apology easier."

Meri crossed her arms. "I didn't do anything wrong."

"Of course not," Anne said. "I'm certain you didn't do anything wrong. Kaylin is just a horrible person who attacks the innocent."

Somehow that didn't feel right either. "She was nice when we were friends," Meredith said. "We used to love all the same books."

Anne nodded. "That's important in a bosom friend. And I do love all your books. Could we talk about books now? I especially want to know about the one with the school for wizards. Do they have schools like that where you live? Do you have a pet owl? Can I see it?"

Again Anne's enthusiasm made Meri laugh. She settled in to talk about some of her favorite books with her new bosom friend.

Worries

When Meri slid into her place at the supper table, Judith nudged her. "You look happy," she said. "Did you settle your Kaylin problem?"

Meri's face fell. "No, but I'm going to talk to her about it tomorrow."

"That's an excellent idea," her mom said as she filled plates and passed them. "Talking a problem out is a good first step."

Meri looked around her family's dining room. The table was big and old, and the chairs around it didn't all match. Meri ran her finger over the gouge in the wood right in front of her place. To her, that spot was just part of the table. It was almost friendly, curving slightly like a smile. But she guessed her family might look different to someone who didn't understand.

Thomas shoved a forkful of mashed potatoes into his mouth and said, "Who were you talking to in your room?"

"Ewww," Kat shrieked. "Thomas is spewing potatoes."

"Thomas, don't talk with your mouth full," Mom said mildly.

Thomas swallowed with a big gulp. "So, who were you talking to?"

"No one," Meredith said. "It was just a book."

"You talk to books?" Thomas asked.

"Meredith downloads talking books from the library," Mom said. "And today she bought speakers so she could listen to them without earbuds when she's in her room. Which is fine as long as you don't play them so loud that they disturb anyone."

"They were disturbing me," Thomas announced.

"No they weren't," Judith said. "My room is right next to Meri's and it wasn't that loud. Stop trying to make trouble."

"Yeah," Kat said, poking her brother. "Stop trying to make trouble for us girls."

This led to a loud argument with the twins, and a little bit of potato throwing until Dad made the twins sit in different chairs and not talk. After that, no one asked Meri about her talking book. She was glad. She still didn't know how to explain Anne to her family.

After supper, Meri worked on her homework at the table. Even though the house had a tiny office with a computer, everyone seemed to end up at the table whenever they had homework. She'd considered working on it in her room, but she knew she'd just end up chatting with Anne. She didn't want Mrs. Miller mad at her for not getting her work done.

"You must have had a lot of homework," her Dad said as he looked up from his own work. "You don't usually end up at the table after supper."

"I didn't start right after school," Meredith said quietly. "I'll be done soon."

Her dad chuckled. "I'm sure you will. When it comes to you and homework, I don't worry. You're not like the rest of this wild crew." He looked fondly toward the kitchen, where Thomas and Kat were arguing over how to load the dishwasher.

Meredith flashed her dad a smile, but she felt a pinch of worry. Was it weird that she always did her homework? Could the mean girls be right? She turned back to her homework, but the worry stayed with her like a poke in her stomach.

The next day, Anne watched Meri as she rushed around getting her stuff together for school. "Now don't forget to talk to your nemesis today," Anne said. "And then tell me all about it when you get home."

Meredith glanced at the mirror. "I still don't think Kaylin is exactly a nemesis."

"She sounds like she has all the potential of becoming a true nemesis," Anne insisted.

"I'll talk to her," Meri said, though she really didn't like confronting people.

When she got to her classroom, she slunk to her seat with her head low so she didn't see Kaylin. She quickly opened her book and began reading. She was glad when Mrs. Miller passed out the morning work packet and she *couldn't* talk to Kaylin.

8

Secret Friends

Meri focused on her work more than ever so she didn't have to think about the talk. By the time reading groups were called together, she felt sick.

"Are you okay?" Jasmine asked softly.

"My stomach hurts a little," Meri admitted.

David leaned forward eagerly, his face excited. "Maybe you should go to the nurse. In my brother's class in middle school, this kid had a stomachache for days and finally something exploded inside him."

Meri looked at him doubtfully, wondering if all boys liked crazy stories.

"No really," David said. "The kid almost died. My brother told me."

"I'm not going to have an explosion," Meri said.

David looked a little disappointed, but he shrugged. Then he asked her if she bought the speakers they'd talked about.

"I did," she said. "They worked great. Thanks for telling me about them."

He gave another shrug, looking a little embarrassed. "That's good." He squirmed in his seat and his cheeks turned pink. "Hey, if you two wanted to play kickball with us at recess, that would be okay. The guys don't mind playing with girls."

Meredith smiled. "Thanks but I'm not really good at kickball."

"Me either," Jasmine said in her whispery voice.

"Neither is Blake," David said. "Yesterday, he tried to kick the ball and missed and flew right over it and landed on his bottom. He didn't get hurt so it was funny. Anyway, you don't have to be good at it."

Meri looked at David. He had a nice, happy face with brown eyes that always seemed full of smiles. And he could read really well, even if he did pick books with strange boy jokes. And his black curls were even wilder than Meri's blonde ones.

"Thanks," she said, meaning it. "I don't think I want to play, but I like being asked."

David looked embarrassed again and jumped out of his seat. "I need to sharpen my pencil. I'll be right back."

Jasmine giggled softly after David walked away. "Kickball," she whispered and giggled again. "He's nice, but silly."

Meri nodded. She thought that described him perfectly. "My sister was this huge kickball champion," she said. "I'm not really good at sports."

"Me either," Jasmine said. "I take karate. I like that."

Meredith looked at the tiny, shy girl curiously. "Wow."

"I'm not really good at it," Jasmine said. "But my parents thought it would help me be less shy."

"Did it?" Meri asked.

Jasmine shrugged. "Not really, but I still like doing it."

Meri didn't know what to say. She couldn't imagine shy Jasmine in karate class. But she wouldn't have expected David to ask her to play with him at recess either. School was strange today.

"It's so nice that you have a big sister," Jasmine said. "I wish I did."

"I have two big sisters. Sometimes it's nice," Meri said. "And sometimes they make me crazy."

Jasmine giggled. "My baby brother is like that."

"My little brother drives me crazy!" Meri said. "He's always fighting with my little sister Kat. They're twins."

"Wow, how many brothers and sisters do you have?" Jasmine asked.

"Three sisters, one brother," Meri said, suddenly worried. Would Jasmine think her family was weird, too?

"That's so cool. I only have one brother and he still wears diapers. I think a big family would be great," Jasmine said with a smile. Meri smiled back.

Beyond them, she saw Mrs. Miller looking at their reading table. Her teacher gave her a sunny smile and a thumbs-up. Meri wasn't sure what she'd done right, but she realized her stomach hardly hurt at all.

When Mrs. Miller announced lunchtime, Meri trudged to the coatroom for her lunch bag, even though she didn't feel much like eating. She didn't think it was a good idea to talk to Kaylin during lunch when everyone would be listening and watching. She really needed to talk to Kaylin all by herself.

Meri nibbled the corner off her sandwich, her eyes on Kaylin. Then the perfect chance arrived. Kaylin was done with her lunch, and she gathered her trash. Meri knew that her ex-friend always went to the restroom and pulled her hair back into a ponytail before going outside.

She'd done it ever since second grade. Kaylin had her ears pierced for her birthday. On her first day with earrings, the wind tangled her hair around the earring post. Untangling her hair from her sore ear made Kaylin cry. Ever since, she always wore a ponytail outside so she wouldn't get tangled again.

Meri watched as Kaylin split off from Gina and Megan and headed toward the door to the hallway. Meri took a deep breath and hurried out. She walked quietly so Kaylin wouldn't turn around and see her.

She followed her ex-friend right through the door of the restroom. "Kaylin, I want to ask you something."

Startled, Kaylin spun around. "What do you want?"

"Why are you so mean to me?" Meri asked. "We used to be friends. We had fun together. My mom even made you her special scratch chocolate pound cake for your birthday. Don't you care about that?"

Kaylin shrugged again, but she looked less sure of herself. "I'm not that mean. I don't say anything that isn't kind of true. You do read a lot. It's all you do."

"It's not all I do," Meri said. "And I thought you loved going to the library together and picking out books and reading stories together."

"I did like that. But I had to do everything else by myself. That's not fun."

"And hanging out with the meanest girls at school is fun?" Meri asked.

"Megan has dance class with me. Gina is on my soccer team," Kaylin said. "We do things."

"You dumped me because I don't like soccer and my family can't afford dance lessons?"

"No," Kaylin said. "But did you know how weird we looked, reading all the time? Megan and Gina thought we were weirdos."

"But now they just think I'm a weirdo?"

Kaylin shrugged, but she looked guilty. "I told them I just did all that reading to make you happy."

"So you had to lie to get different friends?" Meredith said, confused. "And you like girls who called you weird more than you like me?"

"Not more, just different," Kaylin said, her voice turning eager. "Look, I do miss hanging out with you sometimes. We could still be friends when no one is around. I could come over or something. We'd be secret friends."

"And when Megan and Gina are around, you'll still say mean things," Meri said.

"I have to," Kaylin said. "But you'll know I don't really mean it. That's part of the secret."

"You know, if I went for that I really would be weird." Meri shook her head and turned, pushing the doors open and walking away.

Frenemies

The moment Meri sat in front of the mirror, Anne exploded in questions. "Did you talk to your nemesis? What did she say? Do you want my help preparing your apology?"

"I'm not apologizing," Meri said.

Anne's face fell. "Oh, I was working on apology phrases all day." She held up a sheet of paper covered in her looping cursive. The page was a rainbow of apologies.

Meredith scanned the list and recognized phrases from Anne's funny apology to Mrs. Lynde. *I could never express all my sorrow, no, not if I used up a whole dictionary. You must just imagine it.* And *I deserve to be punished and cast out by respectable people forever.*

Meredith smiled. "Thank you for making this list. It makes me feel better."

Anne beamed. "Oh, I am ever so glad. Do you think you will use some of them in your apology?"

"I'm not apologizing," Meri said again. When she saw Anne was about to launch into a speech, Meri quickly added, "She offered to be my friend again as long as we keep it secret."

"Secret friends?" Anne said, her eyes wide. "That sounds so mysterious. Are you going to do it?"

Meredith shook her head. "She just means she's going to be mean to me around her new friends, but nice when no one is around. That's not a friend."

"Oh, no," Anne agreed. "That is a betrayal of all that friendship means. Oh, what a wicked girl to even say that. I do not like her."

"I did talk to David and Jasmine today," Meri said. "They're in my reading group.

They're nice. Jasmine likes to read too, but she's shy."

"I think when someone is shy, they seem so very tragic and soulful. Does she have soulful eyes? I always thought I would love to have soulful eyes."

"I don't think I paid that much attention to her eyes," Meredith said as she laughed again. "How about you? Did you have a good day?"

Anne nodded, though without much cheer. "I do wish I could go to school with you or that school did not last so very long," she said. "I imagine a good deal, and that helps to pass the time. Of course, it's rather lonesome. But then, I may get used to that in time. I must admit, I miss Marilla and Matthew most painfully."

"Oh," Meredith said. She hadn't thought about how horrible it must be to stay trapped all day. She knew that Anne was sent to her room in the book as punishment. Was Meredith punishing her too?

"There's a boy in my school who is a mean, hateful boy. He actually called me 'Carrots,' so I hit him with my slate. Do tell me that this David is not so bold and unkind," Anne said.

"No, David's nice," Meri said. Then, she remembered how much Anne eventually liked the boy in the book. She added, "Though I think you'll find that boys aren't so bad."

"The boy who called me 'Carrots' hurt my feelings excruciatingly."

"He just wants your attention."

Anne huffed and launched into a long explanation of exactly what kind of behavior would get her attention. They ended in a fit of giggles and Meredith thought no more about whether it was right to leave Anne in the mirror.

At school the next day, Meri sat at her table leafing through her book, wondering again what she should do. She couldn't imagine sending Anne back to Green Gables. She would have no friend at all then.

"Oh look, the bookworm is sad."

Meri looked up sharply into Gina's smirky face. "Just go away."

"Wow, that's so snappy, Meredaffy," Megan said.

To Meri's surprise, Kaylin stepped between her friends. "Come on," she said. "Leave Meredith alone."

Gina and Megan looked at her in shock, their mouths open.

"We've got better things to do," Kaylin said, waving a teen fashion magazine at them.

"Oh, okay," Megan said. "Bye, Meredaffy."

Meri watched the three walk back to their worktable.

"You look worried," Jasmine said, slipping into the chair beside her.

"Kaylin is being less mean," Meri said. "We used to be friends, then not really friends. Now I'm not sure what we are."

"It sounds like you are frenemies!" Jasmine said.

10

Saying Good-bye

Meredith looked at Jasmine curiously.

"I read about it in a book. Frenemies aren't friends or enemies—they're tricky. You have to keep an eye on them," Jasmine explained.

"I'll have to do that," Meri agreed.

"I had something else I wanted to ask you," Jasmine added. Her voice dropped to her usual shy whisper.

"What's that?" Meri asked.

Jasmine looked down at the desk and rubbed a finger against a stray pencil mark, smearing it. "My family is going to the zoo this weekend. I was wondering if you might like to go. My mom said it was okay to ask you."

Meri tried to remember if her family had plans for the weekend. As she paused, Jasmine looked upset. She pulled her braid toward her mouth, but didn't quite put it in.

"What's the matter?" Meri asked in alarm.

"I know the zoo is kind of babyish," Jasmine whispered. "It's okay if you don't want to go."

"Of course I do," Meri said. "It'll be fun to go with a friend."

"Are we friends?" Jasmine asked.

"Sure, we both love reading and we have wild little brothers, even if yours is littler than mine. I think we should be friends."

Jasmine smiled. "I've never had a friend to do things with before. It's fun to talk about books in our reading group, but going to the zoo, that's special."

Meredith thought about that. She and Kaylin really hadn't done much together that wasn't about books. Maybe Kaylin did need friends who could do different things. But she still didn't have to be so mean. Meredith was sure about that.

"Are you okay?" Jasmine asked.

"Yes," Meredith said. "Just thinking about something totally different. I'll ask my mom about the zoo today."

Mrs. Miller came to the table with their morning work packets. "Would you like to sit in this seat now, Jasmine?" she asked.

"If that's okay," Jasmine said.

"As long as you both focus on your work during work time," Mrs. Miller said with a smile. "I know how hard it can be not to chatter with friends."

Meri and Jasmine smiled brightly at each other, happy that Mrs. Miller could see they were friends. "We'll focus," Meredith promised.

Jasmine nodded in agreement and Mrs. Miller gave them both their morning work. With just one more grin at each other, both girls settled down to their work.

When she reached the page for the word problem, Meri smiled and wrote: "Jane had

one friend. Then her friend made two other friends, but dropped Jane. So Jane made a magic friend. Then she made a regular friend. How many friends were there all together?"

During every break at school, Jasmine and Meri told each other more things about their families and their favorite things. Meri wondered if she should tell about the magic mirror, but she decided that was something you had to see. She would show Jasmine someday soon.

Thinking about the mirror made Meri worry about Anne. The more she thought about it, the more she knew that it wasn't fair to make Anne stay stuck in Meredith's mirror room all day. Anne was a girl who needed to be outside. She needed to be with all her friends.

When Meri came home, she raced up the stairs and hurried into her room. Anne was sitting at her mirror desk, concentrating on something. Meri slipped into the desk chair and Anne looked up with a smile. The smile was warm, but it didn't light up her eyes like Meri knew it should.

"I think you need to go back to Green Gables," Meri said.

"I don't know how," Anne said, her voice sad. "The windows won't open in here and neither will the doors. I look out the windows but the view is so blurry. I can't even see if there are flowers."

"I think I know how," Meri said. "I think if I take your book off my desk and put it back in the bookcase, you'll get to go home."

"Oh, do you really think so?" Anne said, hope blooming on her face. "How perfectly lovely! You *are* able to imagine things just exactly like me, or else you'd never have understood how I've longed to go home."

Meri nodded. "I'll miss you."

"And I will miss you, truly and dreadfully. Oh, Meredith, I just realized I cannot possibly go home. Not when your nemesis is still being so unkind. How would that be for a bosom friend to behave? I shall have to stay, even though it harrows up my soul. I'd let myself be torn limb from limb if it would do you any good."

"It's okay. I made a friend at school today," Meri said, smiling. "Her name is Jasmine. She doesn't have your imagination, but she loves books. She invited me to the zoo with her family."

"What's a zoo?" Anne asked, her face bright with curiosity.

"It's a place where all kinds of animals live," Meredith said. "There are lions and tigers and elephants and giraffes."

"Oh my." Anne put her hands to her cheeks. "I cannot even imagine. Is it a very dangerous place?"

Meri laughed out loud. "No, the animals are in cages. Nice cages with lots of room."

Anne drooped. "But still, a cage. It is terrible to be trapped, even in a nice place."

"I know," Meri said. "And that's why you have to go home. I have to let you go, even though I'll miss you. But I'll always be your friend."

"Oh, we must make it official," Anne said. "We'll swear it and then it will be true forever and ever." She raised her hand and placed it against the glass of the mirror. "I solemnly swear to be faithful to my bosom friend, Meredith Mercer, as long as the sun and moon shall endure. Now you say it and put my name in the oath."

Meri pressed her hand against the cool mirror glass, directly on top of Anne's. "I solemnly swear to be faithful to my bosom friend, Anne Shirley, as long as the sun and moon shall endure."

"Oh, I believe you," Anne said. "I believe you truly will. Do put my book back in front of the mirror now and then. It will be like having visits. We can pretend we're taking tea. Wouldn't that be lovely?"

"It would," Meri agreed. "You've been a huge help to me, Anne."

"Then I am glad for every minute I've spent," Anne said. "Even when I was alone. Even when I missed Diana and Marilla and Matthew."

Meredith carefully took her copy of *Anne of Green Gables* from the desk and carried it back to slip it into her bookcase. She turned around quickly and saw that Anne was already fading from the mirror. Her friend waved wildly, her eyes bright with tears. Meri waved back, blinking against the stinging in her own eyes.

Finally, the only thing Meri saw in the mirror was her own pale face surrounded by wild blonde curls. She smiled a little at the image, then took a deep breath and turned to head downstairs. She was about to ask her Mom about going to the zoo with her new bosom friend, Jasmine.

About the Author

Jan Fields grew up loving stories where exciting and slightly impossible things happened to ordinary kids like her. She still loves reading stories like that, so she writes books for children looking for the same things.

When she's not writing, Jan pokes around the New England countryside in search of inspiration, magic mirrors, and fairies.